I AM READING

Wakefield Libraries
& Information Services

This book should be returned by the last date stamped above. You may renew the loan personally, by post or telephone for a further period if the book is not required by another reader.

ANTHONY LEWIS

KINGFISHER

An imprint of Kingfisher Publications Plc
New Penderel House, 283-288 High Holborn
London WC1V 7HZ
www.kingfisherpub.com

First published by Kingfisher 1996
This edition published 2004
2 4 6 8 10 9 7 5 3 1

Educational Adviser: Prue Goodwin
Reading and Language Centre
University of Reading

A CIP catalogue record for this book is available from the British Library.

ISBN 0 7534 1045 1

Printed in India
1TR/0604/AJT/(FR)/115MA

Contents

Chapter One
The Beach

Kit was in the mood to make something.

"A castle," he said.

"That's what we need on this beach."

"A castle?" said his little sister, Anna.

"Exactly," said Kit.

"A castle so big and so grand everyone will think of the Olde

"As big and as grand as that?" Anna gasped.

"Well, nearly," said Kit.

He set to work with his bucket and spade.

Chush! Chush! Chush!

Anna sat on a rock, watching.

Kit's castle didn't look

very big and grand to her

– not even nearly.

"What's that, Kit?" she asked.

"It's a moat," Kit said.

"A castle needs water all round the outside

to keep the bad people out."

"That's right," said Anna.

"I remember now."

"Do you?" Kit smiled.

He'd forgotten the picture

at Granny's house.

It showed a castle so magnificent,

the moat was like a river.

People could swim in it, if they liked,

or go boating.

Next, Kit tipped up some buckets of sand.

He built towers all round the castle

with walls in between.

His spade kept everything

smooth and flat.

Pat! Pat! Pat!

Anna watched as he finished off.

"What are those things there?"

she pointed.

"These bumps on top of the towers,

Anna?

They're called battlements.

And these slits in the walls are windows."

"Thanks for reminding me," said Anna.

"Reminding you?" Kit frowned.

He'd forgotten the book from the library.

It showed a castle so splendid

it had bumps and slits all over it

and hundreds of soldiers as well.

Now Kit was fiddling with string

and cardboard and lollysticks

– and dollops of gum to fix them;

Blob! Blob! Blob!

Anna's eyes lit up.

"Aren't they called . . ."

"This is a drawbridge,"

Kit told her.

"See how it lifts up and down

to keep everyone safe in the castle?

So does this grid-thing.

It's called a portcullis."

"Of course," Anna nodded.

"I'm glad you agree," sniffed Kit.

By now he was cross with her.

He thought she was just pretending.

He'd forgotten the film

they'd both seen on television.

It showed a drawbridge so huge

it looked like a flap for a giant cat.

The portcullis was huge, too.

It had spiky bits just like teeth.

Kit filled in the moat with water.

He stuck flags on the towers.

He put soldiers from his toybox

all round the castle.

"There," he said.

"Now it's as good as the Olden Days."

"Well, nearly," said Anna.

"Nearly?" said Kit.

"What do you mean, nearly?"

"No dungeon yet," said Anna.

"That's a room deep, deep,

down in the castle, Kit,

where you lock people up."

"I'll make one," said Kit.

"And a keep?" Anna asked.

"That's the tallest part of the castle

where the rich people live."

"I'll have one of those, too,"

Kit promised.

"And stables, Kit?

And a kitchen?

And a blacksmith's to mend their swords?"

"No problem," said Kit in surprise.

"Hey, you sound like a castle expert, Anna.

How do you know all this stuff?"

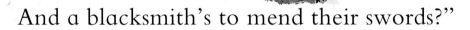

Anna thought of the film on television,
the book from the library
and the picture on Granny's wall.
"From the Olden Days," she smiled.
Of course, she really was pretending
this time.

Chapter Two
The Dream

That night, Kit and Anna

slept in the beach house.

They could hear the waves coming in.

Hush . . . they went.

Hush . . .

Then again . . . hush.

The sound was so soft and so comfy,

no wonder Kit had his dream.

All round him was a castle.

It was as big and as grand

as the Olden Days.

"Hey," Kit called.

"Who's the King of this Castle?"

"Nobody," said an old woman.

"Nobody?" said Kit.

"In that case,

will you lend me

that cloak you're mending?"

"Certainly, young sir."

Kit loved the cloak at once.

It was as smart and swirly

as only a dream-cloak can be.

Next he stood in the castle courtyard.

He saw stable-boys feeding horses.

He saw kitchen-girls cooking food.

He saw a blacksmith tending his forge.

"Hey," called Kit.

"Who's the King of this castle?"

"Nobody," said the blacksmith.

"In that case," Kit said,

"will you lend me

that sword you're sharpening?"

"Certainly, young sir."

The sword was as keen and shiny

as only a dream-sword can be.

No wonder Kit wanted to keep it.

In front of him now was a tall, heavy door.

"Who's the King of this castle?" he called.

"Nobody," said the jester

who was practising tricks on the doorstep.

"I see," said Kit.

"In that case,

will you lend me

that ring and that crown

and that necklace you're juggling with?"

"Certainly *not*, young sir."

But the jester was only joking.

The ring and the crown and the necklace

were as golden and glittery

as only dream-treasure can be . . .

That's why Kit couldn't resist them.

At last he was in the Great Hall.

He saw flags high up,

and a huge fireplace,

and carpets that hung on the walls

like pictures.

"These are tapestries," he whispered.

"They're much too special

to put on the floor.

Who looks after all this wonderful stuff?"

"I do, young sir," said the Bailiff.

"It's my job to take care of everything."

Kit took a deep breath.

"In that case," he said,

"who's the King of this castle?"

"Nobody," someone called.

Kit knew that voice.

He turned to the throne by the fire.

There, in her pyjamas,

sat his little sister, Anna.

"Welcome to my castle, young sir,"

she said.

"Your castle?" gasped Kit.
"So this cloak and this sword
and this necklace . . ."
"Belong to me," said Anna.
And the look on her face
was as queenly as only a
dream-queen can be.

Kit couldn't help thinking of dungeons.

Or standing in the stocks.

Or having his head chopped off.

These, too, were part of the Olden Days.

Quickly, he dropped on one knee.

"Here are the royal clothes,

your majesty," he said.

"Shall I help you put them on?"

"Thank you, Kit," smiled the Queen.

After this, the Great Hall was silent.

Hush . . . went the castle.

Hush . . .

Then again . . . hush.

It sounded just like the waves coming in.

Chapter Three
The Competition

Next morning, Kit said,

"Shall we share this castle, Anna?"

"Share it?" said Anna.

"Between us, yes," said Kit.

Anna was too happy to answer.

So now they were both in a castle mood.

After all, it was the only castle

on the beach.

Or was it?

Soon they saw other kids hard at work

— more and more of them.

Everyone had a bucket and spade.

Some had grown-ups helping them, too.

Were they all building castles?

Chush!

Chush!

Chush!

"What's going on?" Kit asked.

"Look!" Anna pointed.

Kit saw a huge banner.

It hung over the sea-front

like a tapestry.

It said:

SANDCASTLE
COMPETITION
TODAY

BUILD THE BEST EVER
CASTLE ON THIS BEACH
WIN A VISIT TO A
REAL-LIFE CASTLE

Anna's eyes sparkled.

"Kit, do you think

our castle might win?"

Kit was wondering that himself.

He looked hard at all the others.

He saw moats and drawbridges

and battlements everywhere.

They were the biggest and best
he'd ever seen.

Nobody was fiddling with string
and cardboard and lollysticks now.
These castles were much too grand.
Sadly, Kit shook his head.
"No chance, Anna.
Anyway, who cares?
People don't live in castles any more.
They cost too much.
Besides, we can knock them down
too easily with tanks
and rockets and bombs."
"Granny told me that," said Anna.
"Most castles are ruins, Anna.
They're just holiday places
for visitors, nowadays."

"Shall we make our castle

into a nowadays castle?"

 Anna suggested.

"Why not?" said Kit.

So that's what they did.

They knocked down the walls a bit.

They knocked down each of the

towers a bit.

They knocked down a bit of the keep

and a bit of the kitchen

and a bit of the blacksmith's.

Then they opened Kit's toybox.

Out came his model village

with its houses and cars and people.

Soon, the castle

had a holiday look to it.

"Visitors everywhere," said Kit.

"So real," Anna agreed.

"And so up to date," came a voice.

It was a smart, friendly lady

with a notebook in her hand.

She walked round the castle,

nodding her head.

Then she walked round again.

Kit couldn't bear it any longer.

"Are you the Judge

of the Sandcastle Competition?"

he asked.

"That's exactly who I am," said the lady.

"They chose me because my job

is taking care of a real-life castle, you see."

"Like a bailiff?"

"Just like a bailiff, yes.

You know, this castle of yours is brilliant.

It's the only one on the beach

that doesn't look new.

I'm so impressed

I'm going to make it the winner."

"The winner!" Kit gasped.

"Does that mean we can visit
your real-life castle?" Anna asked.
"That's the prize, isn't it?"
"It certainly is," said the lady.
"I'll show you all over it myself
– from the deepest dungeon
to the tallest tower."

"You and your brother
will be Queen and King for a day.
What do you think of that?"
"Magic," said Kit, faintly.
"Just like the Olden Days."
"Well, nearly," Anna beamed.

About the Author and Illustrator

Chris Powling has been a teacher and is now editor of the children's book magazine *Books for Keeps*. He has written many novels and stories for children including *The Phantom Carwash*. "I just love visiting castles," says Chris, "though I'm not sure I'd like to have lived in one – they must have been very cold in the winter!"

Anthony Lewis went to the Liverpool College of Art and since graduating has illustrated lots of children's books. Anthony says: "The castle I've visited most recently is Blarney Castle in Ireland. There's a famous stone there and it's said that if you kiss it, you will always have a way with words. I hope it works!"

Tips for Beginner Readers

1. Think about the cover and the title of the book. What do you think it will be about? While you are reading, think about what might happen next and why.

2. As you read, ask yourself if what you're reading makes sense. If it doesn't, try rereading or look at the pictures for clues.

3. If there is a word that you do not know, look carefully at the letters, sounds and word parts that you do know. Blend the sounds to read the word. Is this a word you know? Does it make sense in the sentence?

4. Think about the characters, where the story takes place, and the problems the characters in the story faced. What are the important ideas in the beginning, middle and end of the story?

5. Ask yourself questions like:
  Did you like the story?
  Why or why not?
  How did the author make it fun to read?
  How well did you understand it?

Maybe you can understand the story better if you read it again!